For Karen Kennedy

First published in 1994

1 3 5 7 9 10 8 6 4 2

First published in the United Kingdom in 1994 by
Hutchinson Children's Books
Random House, 20 Vauxhall Bridge Road,
London SW1V 2SA

Random House Australia (Pty) Limited
20 Alfred Street, Milsons Point, Sydney,
New South Wales 2061, Australia

Random House New Zealand Limited
18 Poland Road, Glenfield,
Auckland 10, New Zealand

Random House South Africa (Pty) Limited
PO Box 337, Bergvlei, South Africa

Designed by Paul Welti and Pete Howard

Random House UK Limited Reg. No. 954009

A CIP catalogue record for this book
is available from the British Library

ISBN 0 09 176227 8

Printed in Hong Kong

AS QUIET AS A MOUSE

Hilda Offen

HUTCHINSON
London Sydney Auckland Johannesburg

I was as quiet as a mouse,
I tiptoed around.

Put fingers to lips

Walk on tiptoe

I listened and listened –
there wasn't a sound.

Put hand to ear

Then... a butterfly
breathed a sigh.

Sigh

A worm gave a wiggle
and started to giggle.

'A-choo!' sneezed the hen.
Then she did it again.

Pretend to sneeze

The pig was so bored
that he lay down and snored.

Snore

'Clap your hands, girls and boys!'
cried the seal. 'Make a noise.'

Clap your hands

The chimp said, ‘I’m champ,’
and started to stamp.

Laugh

The bear gave a shout,
'The wolf's coming, look out!'

Shout 'Look out!'

The wolf said, 'I'll huff,
and I'll huff and I'll puff!'

Huff and puff

Then the dinosaur roared,
and he roared and he ROARED!

Roar very loudly

What a terrible din!
What a noise! What a row!

Sigh, giggle, sneeze, snore, clap, stamp, laugh, shout, huff and puff, roar

I jumped on a box
and I yelled, 'Stop it now!'

Shout 'Stop it!'

I made them be quiet,
it didn't take long.

Whisper 'Shhh!'